The

One Hundred Stories,
Of One Hundred Words,
Honouring Those Who
Lived and Died One Hundred
Years Ago.

By
Dawn Knox

To
Mum
Jamie and James
Thank you for believing in me
***

Dad
I miss you and think of you every day
***

With thanks
to
Bob Sheridan
and
Ken Porter
Without you both, this book would never
have been written.
***


To
George Burnett,
Louis Vallin
and
Albert Kiekert.
Men who fought for their countries.
I never met you but you have touched my
life deeply.

# Contents

## Introduction

These one hundred stories of exactly one hundred words, are my tribute to the men and women of all nations, who lived and died during the First World War.

In 2014, Stephen Metcalfe, MP of South Basildon and East Thurrock, launched the *Forget Never, Oublier Jamais, Vergessen Niemals* project, to commemorate the centenary of the beginning of the First World War, which was funded by the Heritage Lottery Fund. I first became interested in the events of 1914 to 1918, when I was asked to write a script for a dramatisation that was to be performed during the Christmas concert - the finale of the year-long project. Basildon's twin towns of Meaux, in France, and Heiligenhaus, in Germany, were both also involved, and I was asked to include a serviceman from each of the three towns in the script. Three men were selected, George Burnett from Wickford, Essex, Louis Vallin from Meaux, and Albert Kiekert from Heiligenhaus.

The international nature of the audience - British, French and German - presented me with a challenge. How could I best portray men who one hundred years ago would have been regarded as the enemy in a sympathetic and believable way? I determined that, as far as I could, I would represent each man equally with no suggestion of winners and losers.

As part of my research, I read Joshua Levine's excellent book, *Forgotten Voices of the Somme: The Most Devastating Battle of the Great War in the Words of Those Who Survived,* and as expected, I found descriptions of atrocities with which I'd associated the Great War, as well as reports of outstanding heroism and bravery. However, to my surprise, I also discovered accounts where friend and foe put aside their enmity and helped each other, in acts of touching compassion.

For the first time, it occurred to me that although the young men who were called on to fight wore different uniforms and spoke different languages, in fact, there were more similarities between them, than differences. This was a theme I was keen to explore and develop, and eventually, the dramatisation, *The Sons of Three Countries Remembered,* was born.

Since then, I have been fascinated by the lives of ordinary people who lived and died during the Great War. I attended a talk by Peter Doyle and Robin Shäfer based on their wonderful book *Fritz and Tommy, Across the Barbed Wire,* which I also read, and I decided to write some very short stories which offered a glimpse into the First World War era. Initially, I planned to write about ten stories, but the ideas kept coming until eventually, I had written one hundred.

I'm not a historian and sadly, I've never had the opportunity to talk to anyone who experienced the war, but I've tried to imagine how people might have reacted to the world in which they found themselves and to speak in their voices.

So, here are one hundred glimpses into the First World War, each written in exactly one hundred words, to honour those who lived one hundred years ago.

With thanks to Joshua Levine, Peter Doyle and Robin Shäfer.

Levine, J. (2008) – Forgotten Voices of the Somme – The Most Devastating Battle of the Great War in the Words of Those Who Survived in Association with the Imperial War Museum, London. Ebury Press and imprint of Ebury Publishing.

Doyle, P. and Shäfer, R. (2015) – Fritz and Tommy Across the Barbed Wire, The History Press, The Mill, Brimscombe Port, Stroud, Gloucestershire, GL5 2QG

# The Start

No one at the time suspected that the assassination of the heir of the Austro-Hungarian Empire, and his wife, would have such tragic repercussions.

Who would have guessed that their murder would be the catalyst which ignited the first truly, global war?

A disaffected young Bosnian Serb, who was a member of a terrorist gang, shot at the Archduke and his wife during a state visit by the royal couple to Sarajevo.

There was no going back.

Country after country declared war and mobilised their troops to take part in what was subsequently named, *The War to End all Wars.*

## Final Words

With blank, unseeing eyes, he stares towards
heaven.
God rest his soul.
I prise the blood-spattered envelope from fingers
that are rigidly clenched over his heart, and I
silently vow to carry his final words home if I
live to see my next leave.
A creased photograph of a young girl slips out
of the letter.
It's *her* heart I'll break when I deliver the
soldier's farewell.
Should I tell her he died alone in a muddy
hollow on French soil, with blood seeping from
his severed leg into the earth?
No, I'll simply say her sweetheart died a hero.

## The Letter

As I open the letter with trembling fingers, I know this moment will change my life forever.

The words are blurry through my tears but unmistakable; *Missing in Action*.

'Mama, there's still hope. It says *missing*, not...' My daughter wraps her arms around me, her young face willing me not to despair.

'We got a letter from him only yesterday telling us he's well.'

But, how many days ago had he written those words?

And how long does it take a bullet to end a life?

My only son.

Missing in action.

How can life ever be the same again?

# The Sniper

A shot. A cry. A thud.

We drop to the ground and freeze.

'Who's down?'

No one dares raise their head to find out.

'Sniper!' the sergeant whispers, 'Where'd the shot come from?' but no one replies.

'Mason, on my word, break cover.'

'Sarge?'

'That's an order.'

Mason leaps to his feet and zigzags between the trees. As a single shot rings out, he drops to his knees.

'Up there, Sarge,' whispers one of the men, and taking aim, he fires into the trees until there is a cry and the enemy sniper falls from his perch.

Three wasted lives.

## Seeking Comfort

The soldiers call her Queenie.

It isn't her name but it pleases her.

She knows they refer to her simple establishment as the *Pleasure Palace* because for a few short hours, they can forget the brutality of war; enjoying food, brandy and girls.

But mostly her girls.

She watches the men sitting on the stairs leading to the bedrooms above, one on each step clutching five francs. In their faces, she sees excitement, fear, hope, and she knows that for some, it will be the first time with a woman.

They live for today because tomorrow may be too late.

## The Touch

'I will not tolerate tears in this hospital,' the
sister tells her nurses. 'Your eyes must be sharp
to check for vital signs.'

Pulse, temperature and respiration.

She teaches them how to assess each
wounded man, separating those who need
immediate attention from those for whom she
can offer nothing more than a gentle word and a
prayer.

The nurses marvel at her ability to tell
from one touch if a man's temperature is due to
the evening chill or whether it foretells imminent
death.

But they turn away and pretend not to see
the sister's tears when they fall.

# Deadly Duet

With knives drawn and eyes locked, the two young soldiers circle each other. It is a micro-battle within a macro-battle, being waged in a deep shell hole somewhere lost in No Man's Land.

Two enemy soldiers have dived into the same hollow to avoid death but the rules of war state that one must die.

They circle, feint, strike and parry, until exhausted, they fall to their knees.

Who is the strongest?

Perhaps they are evenly matched.

Perhaps they have come to respect each other.

Whatever the reason, warily, they sheath their knives, shake hands and return to their comrades.

# (William) George Burnett

(William) George Burnett left his home in Wickford, Essex and sailed to France with the British Expeditionary Force in August 1914.

He left a promising career in the Essex Police Force as a constable, to rejoin the Coldstream Guards as Lance Corporal 7591. The First Battalion Coldstream Guards were not seriously engaged in battle until September, but a month later, during heavy fighting, George Burnett went missing in action.

His body was never found although he is remembered with honour on the Menin Gate.

George Burnett was twenty-three years old when he was killed in action on 29th October 1914.

## Albert Kiekert

Albert Kiekert left his family and legal studies to join his brother, Fritz, in the First Lorraine Field Artillery Regiment.

He was wounded three times in battle and later became an observer in a reconnaissance biplane.

On 27 January 1918, Albert had completed fifteen operational flights when his plane was hit by gunfire at the height of 3,600 metres, and one minute and fifteen seconds later, he and the pilot crashed into the ground not far from Verdun, France.

He was remembered by his officers as being dashing, loyal, and brave.

Albert Kiekert was killed at the age of twenty-five.

# Louis Vallin

Louis Vallin's dream of flying was realised when he joined the French Air Force as a gunner and observer, during which time, he took probably the first aerial shots over his home town of Meaux.

He was honoured for his bravery, being the first pilot to engage in a night fight between an aeroplane and a German Zeppelin, armed only with a rifle and incendiary ammunition.

Louis survived the war, married, and had one daughter.

He determined to do all he could to ensure that flying should be a means of reuniting mankind.

Louis died at the age of 76.

# 01 July

The explosion, when it came, seemed to rock the earth from its axis.

We'd known about the mines tunnelled deep beneath the enemy lines. We'd seen the miners emerge blinking into the daylight, covered in sweat-streaked grime, and we'd known when to expect zero hour.

But no one could possibly have guessed how high the ground would be flung, how many enemy soldiers might be torn apart, or how violently the shockwaves would strike everything that lay in their path, until their rage was spent.

The first day of what would be called *The Battle of the Somme* had begun.

# I Wait

Yesterday I lay in wait.

My comrades and I were ready to ambush the enemy.

Patiently, we longed for, yet dreaded the call to advance, while we spoke to each other silently, using eye contact only.

We encouraged, with smiles and winks.

We silently promised to carry news to the loved ones of those who didn't survive the day.

We prayed.

Then, at the signal, we hurled ourselves at the enemy.

Now, frightened and exhausted, only yards from the safety of the ditch where I hid yesterday, I'm alone and wounded.

My end is near and I lie in wait.

# A Man

'I'm not afraid,' the boy whispers through teeth that chatter louder than his words.

Eyes wide and nostrils flared, he grips the rifle tightly. The blood supply to his dirt-encrusted fingernails is stopped, turning them white.

There's no point telling him not to worry.

Our trench is bathed in blood and the stench of decay is in our nostrils.

Death is near.

What matters now, is not when, but how our lives end. That's all we have left.

The determination to be brave.

How tragic, the boy who didn't live long enough to become a man, will die a man.

## Outstanding Courage

Armed with a revolver, the officer climbs over the parapet and marches, as if on parade, across the ravages of No Man's Land.

Friendly eyes follow his progress, wide in disbelief, whilst enemy eyes line him up in their rifle sights.

He's aware of the danger, but bravely strides towards the injured infantryman hanging wounded and broken on the barbed wire.

Such an easy target.

But as the officer disentangles the soldier and carries him to safety on his shoulder, cheering is heard from the enemy lines.

And there, amidst the slaughter, enemies forget their differences and salute outstanding courage.

40

## Pal's Company

How proud we were as we marched out of the factory gates!

How confident that we would singlehandedly beat the Hun!

And how loudly the womenfolk cheered us as we paraded through town.

Managers, office workers, machine operators; men with different abilities and backgrounds but with one thing in common, we were pals.

And as we marched, more men left their shops and homes to join us, caught up in the patriotic fever.

It occurred to me that the town would be remarkably quiet when we'd gone.

But it wouldn't be long until we'd won the war and returned home.

## Leaving Today

We lie with bodies entwined, whispering until the first light slides unbidden and unwelcome into our room.

Today, my husband, my lover, my friend, and my life will leave to join his regiment.

He will not return for some time, perhaps ever.

So, now, we cling to each other, speaking of our love and of shared memories, both good and bad. But we are careful to avoid mentioning the future.

All plans are now on hold.

Dreams must not be dreamed until he is back safely in my arms again.

It is time.

He leaves and something inside me dies.

## My Conscience

His eyes narrow in anger.

Her mouth curls in contempt.

It doesn't matter how strong my beliefs nor how noble, no one in this military tribunal will judge me fairly.

He thumps the table with his fist as he talks of *patriotism*, *civic duty*, and of course, *cowardice*.

She nods and the other members of the tribunal mutter in agreement.

But I cannot, and will not agree to kill or maim. It is against my conscience. I will give account of myself on the Day of Judgement, and stand tall, as I do now.

Then God will be my judge.

## Facing Facts

I don't need a mirror to see my disfigurement. The fleeting look of revulsion and pity on the face of the nurse when she removed the bandages was sufficient.

I remember the explosion and being carried out of the trench on a stretcher; my face a mass of blood and smashed bone.

I don't know how long I've lain here, in darkness, swathed in bandages wracked with such pain I wanted to die.

Now I have *healed*. Much of my face is missing but I shall not look on it with my own eye.

I know how hideous I am.

## Canary Girl

Yellow skin and hair.

Like a creature from a different planet.

But she is just an ordinary girl, a factory worker who uses TNT, to make shells for her country's army. She is searched on her way in to work and anything that might cause a spark such as a hairpin is taken from her. One spark could send the factory sky high.

And for this dangerous work, she will turn bright yellow and may suffer headaches, rashes and chest infections.

She is doing a man's job for lower wages than a man would earn, for love of her country.

# Death Day

One man arrives in the trenches. He is young, strong and eager to engage in battle. He is warned to keep his head down but it is so easy to forget this order when you're young, strong and eager to engage in battle.

Within minutes, the young soldier is dead.

Another man arrives, keen to make his mark.

He runs onto No Man's Land, dodging bullets as he drags wounded comrades to safety.

The hero is unscathed.

How can this be?

I can only assume that each man has an allotted day to die.

Will today be my Death Day?

# The Dugout

The earth shudders as the shelling reaches a deafening crescendo. The walls of the trench subside and the dugout collapses as timbers crack, and corrugated iron sheets bend beneath the weight of soil.

Seconds before, the soldier would have been crawling into the hole, and the roof would have caved in, smothering him. But he had turned round, and now, his face is only partially covered with earth.

Men desperately dig him out before he suffocates, dragging his limp body from the debris.

He is alive.

But from now on, he will never know a night's sleep without a nightmare.

## Faithful Friend

He's small, wiry, and lightning fast, just like my dog, at home.

The men call him *Lucky*.

He's been trained to carry messages between the lines and if one of the enemy approaches, he silently lays low and pricks up his ears, warning us.

Somehow, he seems to be able to distinguish between our men and the enemy, and many times, he's led us into No Man's Land to rescue wounded soldiers.

Lucky is our mascot.

He is so well loved; several men have volunteered to take messages in his place so that our faithful friend can remain with us.

# The Shame

Within days of arriving in the trenches, I lost the sight in one eye and have limited vision in the other, so now, I serve my King and country in a munitions factory.

I would love to rejoin my fellow soldiers, but I am useless to them with such poor sight.

My scars have healed, and I appear to be able-bodied, so I'm regularly targeted by women of the White Feather Movement, who have presented me with three white feathers in as many months.

My explanations fall on deaf ears.

Each white feather is an arrow that pierces my heart.

## More Men

Men go over the top, they march across No Man's Land, they fall, and the lucky ones crawl back to be patched up so they can do it again.

There is no time to count them and if there were time, I wouldn't want to know.

One day, someone will estimate the numbers of wounded, dead and missing and the world will cry out in agony.

In the meantime, as men die and are lost, more arrive.

I ask myself if one day, there will be no men left.

Will a whole generation of young men have been wiped out?

## Gas Cloud

We wait, hardly daring to breathe, to see where the wind will carry the dense, green cloud. Through condensation inside our goggles, we watch as the gas hovers ominously over No Man's Land. Each soldier has a pad soaked in sodium bicarbonate in place over nose and mouth, but it is hard to believe that such a simple measure will protect us from the chlorine gas that is edging its way closer.

I want to urge my men not to lose their nerve but I must not remove the pad to speak.

The wind picks up and we are engulfed.

# Gas Mask

Heavy shelling usually accompanies a gas attack, so when the alarm went last night, we put on gas helmets and hurried back to our billets.

The goggles steamed up making it impossible to see where we were going. I fell down shell holes and ran into trees, and by the time I got back to the billet, I couldn't bear the helmet any longer, so I ripped it off.

If there'd been gas present, I would have died.

My sweat had activated some of the chemicals impregnated in the helmet and they burned my forehead.

I think I'm permanently scarred.

# Daddy's Home

When Daddy was away, Mummy missed him so much, she cried every day.

But now my Daddy's home.

At least I think it's Daddy; he looks thinner and older than I remember.

He doesn't swing me up on to his shoulders any more. And he doesn't take me for walks by the river.

I have to be quiet while he's resting, although I don't know why he's so tired during the day. Sometimes I hear him shouting at night when he should be asleep.

I thought Mummy would be happy when he came home but she still cries every day.

# Killing Machines

Sweat-soaked inside the oppressive heat of the tank, and nauseous from the exhaust fumes, we fire shot after shot until we are standing knee deep in empty shell cases.

The caterpillar tracks of the tank bite deeply into the earth dragging us forward; a large armoured beast that can cross any trench or crater.

We mow down the barbed wire that covers No Man's Land, crushing it into the soil.

To those who have never seen our armoured tanks, we must be terrifying indeed.

Enormous, unstoppable killing machines that emerge out of the mist and destroy all in their path.

## Marching, Marching

The rhythm is well established. We've been marching for hours or possibly days along muddy roads.

I felt tired hours ago but now I am beyond exhaustion.

I follow the man in front, keeping my eyes on his back so I don't lose him in the dark.

There is silence broken only by the occasional curse as a soldier stumbles.

I don't allow myself the luxury of thought, otherwise how could I bear the weight of my machine gun or the straps of my backpack cutting into my shoulders?

The steady rhythm of our boots says rest, rest, rest, rest.

# The Coward

So, this is it.

The moment I've been dreading.

We wait for the signal to go over the top, poised with bayonets fixed to our rifles, lined up at the side of the trench.

I'm breathing so fast, I fear I might faint but I'm driven on by the memory of my father with his hands at my throat, threatening to kill me himself if I show weakness on the battlefield.

When the whistle sounds, will my legs work?

Will they do as I command and propel me over the top?

Or will I be the disappointment my father fears?

# The Padre

I am a man of God and when I'm sober, I tell all who will listen that God is on our side.

But a drink or two allows unbidden thoughts to infiltrate my consciousness and I wonder if God is weeping at the wanton destruction of those He has created, and if He is angry that both we, and our enemy, claim exclusive rights to his favour and blessing.

Why would He choose one man over another because of his birthplace?

Shouldn't I preach that He loves all men equally?

And yet I claim that He is on our side.

## From Above

The pilot turns to me and points out something far beneath our plane. His words are snatched by the wind and lost amongst the clouds but I can see what he is drawing my attention to.

Below are the trenches, both ours and the enemy's, etched into the earth in seemingly random fashion.

The buffer zone between them is now barely visible.

Bombardment from the front lines is so fierce that smoke hangs over No Man's Land like dirty cotton wool.

Shells explode and flash, like sequins.

We are so remote flying above the clouds, but below, men are dying.

## A Rest

After nine days on the front line, with Death our constant companion, we were more than ready for a break.

A five mile march from the trenches brought us to a small town, bedraggled and exhausted, but happy.

My pals and I were billeted with a fine family and last night, we slept on dry mattresses, not fearing an attack.

Today, I washed and shaved for the first time in days and after cleaning my ammunition, sword and rifle, there was drill and an hour's march.

Moving back to the line with all its dangers will come all too soon.

## Keeping Clean

The soldier loudly curses the lice that swarm over his body, sucking his blood and leaving blotchy, red marks that itch and irritate.

He queues patiently for a bath, hoping the disinfectant in the vat will wash the creatures away.

About one hundred men will bathe in the same water before a fresh bath is prepared.

The eighty-nine soldiers before him have left their grime behind.

Once clean, he will be issued with new clothes and underlinen and have a brief respite from lice.

Back in the trenches, the lice are waiting. He will be infested again in no time.

## My Son

His hair is dark, just like his father's and with trembling fingers, I stroke his downy head. My touch, although almost imperceptible, is enough to waken him.

My newborn son, barely an hour old.

Born into a world at war.

Born to a doting mother and a father who is missing in action, somewhere in France.

I look into my baby's eyes and feel such love welling up inside me that I can scarcely contain it, and such terrible fears for the future.

Tucking my finger in his tiny fist, I whisper, 'Will you ever meet your father, my son?'

## Still Alive

Our sons marched away together in a pal's battalion, young, determined and enthusiastic.

Their lives on hold while they did their bit for king and country.

They trained together, fought together and ultimately, many of them died together.

But not my son.

My son lost an arm.

But he is safe.

His days in the trenches are over and I thank God for bringing him back to me.

When I'm in town, I know other mothers watch me, aware that I still have my boy and that they will never see theirs again.

I cannot look them in the eyes.

## Singing Together

There is still a hint of light in the sky but there will not be a moon tonight, and soon, we will be immersed in darkness.

I take my harmonica and start to play a lively tune.

A soldier further along the trench starts to sing the chorus and others join in. Someone beats a rhythm with a spoon on a mess tin.

Voices drift across No Man's Land, singing words in a different language, but to the same music, and we all sing together.

Enemies harmonising.

The song ends and I start a mournful melody.

The trenches fall silent.

## Take Him

While he is at the pub, I take a pen and paper.

With luck, I will have time to post the letter before he returns.

I need luck.

If he finds out about the letter I have planned, he will beat me black and blue.

Again.

Next week, he will appear at the military tribunal, pleading for exemption from conscription.

He will claim his wife, children and parents rely on his butcher's shop to survive. I will write anonymously and let the tribunal know I run the shop while he drinks the profits.

I will beg them to take him.

## Guilty Hands

She's tempted to throw his unread letter away. It will be the same as all the others, expressing his love and his longing for her and his plans for their future.

A few days ago, the hands that once caressed her, held this letter while he wrote. As it lies in her hands, it is almost as if he is touching her, through time and across the miles.

She wonders if he can feel her guilt.

She didn't mean to fall in love with another.

She doesn't want to break his heart while he's homesick, fighting in a foreign land.

## My Prayer

Dear God,

I hope you don't mind me sending this prayer.

I know I haven't had much time for you in the past so I don't blame you if you don't want to hear, but Padre says you listen to everyone.

You're probably busy at the moment with the war and everything, and I know I don't really deserve any of your time but if you could just see your way clear to looking out for me and the lads today, I'd be mighty glad.

There's going to be heavy fighting today, and we could do with some help.

Amen

# Photographic Record

There are no officers in sight; just me and the lads.

I get my Vest Pocket Kodak Camera out and opening the front, I slide the lens panel forward along the runners. Once the settings are adjusted, I peer through the viewfinder at the lads.

They pose, raising their mugs and larking about as I click my way through the film.

I've heard it said that soldiers can get court-martialled and shot if they're found with a camera, but our officers are decent chaps and I'll be careful.

One day, people will want to know what happened in the trenches.

## Making Music

My mate has gone to get help.

But it's taking so long.

If only I could have crawled with him, back across No Man's Land, but my leg is so bad, it was out of the question.

The sun was much lower when I was hit and now it's directly overhead, so I know I've been here for hours.

The only thing that's keeping me sane is imagining I'm playing my saxophone.

I can see the notes on the musical score and I play them in my mind.

I can hear the music in my head, like a gramophone record.

# Flying Ace

For the forty-fourth time, the pilot watches as an enemy plane spirals out of the sky, leaving a trail of black smoke lingering on the breeze.

An explosion marks the end of its fall.

He has scored another aerial victory and now can claim more than two strikes for every year of his life.

Aged twenty, he should have many years ahead of him, but as a pilot, he will be lucky to survive a few more weeks.

So far, he has shown flair, courage and shrewdness but one lapse in concentration will see him shot out of the sky.

# The Conchie

'Whose side are you bloody conchies on?' the Sergeant yells at us.

No one replies.

There's no point.

No one has sympathy for the plight of the members of the Non-Combatant Corps.

It doesn't matter how much earth I move with my shovel, how many rocks I break with my pick, or how many lorries I load or unload; I am despised.

I wear a uniform; I follow orders but I refuse to bear arms.

I will not kill or wound a fellow human, and yet, I am treated worse than a common murderer by those who support the war.

## Land Girls

We're slowly gaining the farmer's confidence and trust. Our enthusiasm and cheerfulness have compensated for lack of knowledge or experience.

We've been quick to learn, and we work together when one girl's strength is insufficient.

Some might think the work is dirty, cold, tiring and tedious, but we know the food we produce is vital to the war effort.

And I'd rather spend my days in the fresh air, than being poisoned by toxic fumes in a munitions factory.

We, of the Women's Land Army, salute our fighting men, and are proud to be doing *our* bit for this country.

## Trench Rats

If I get out of this war alive, I will never be able to forget the trench rats.

A shiver of revulsion goes through me, when I recall the constant rattling of the tin cans we discard on No Man's Land, as rats feast on food remnants.

They've grown so bold, they steal food from our plates and run over our faces in the night when we finally manage to grab a few minutes sleep.

But my nightmares will always be filled with the sight of rats gorging on a dead man's eyes before devouring the rest of the corpse.

## At Dawn

I've written to my mother, telling her I love her and begging her forgiveness, although I can't bring myself to tell her that at dawn, I'll face the firing squad.

Others will inform her, and she will live with the shame of having a coward for a son.

But I'm not a coward and I don't believe I deserted, despite what the court martial said.

I volunteered for service and have fought bravely; ask anyone.

But recently, I seem to be suffering memory lapses.

I can't remember where I've been or what I've done.

If I'd deserted, wouldn't I know?

## Firing Squad

I could not hold back the tears as I aimed my rifle at the blindfolded deserter. This wasn't what I'd joined the army for.

Our target was the white handkerchief over his heart.

When the order came, I aimed wide and as the gun smoke cleared, we saw that all but one of us had missed.

He was bleeding and struggling against the ropes that bound him to a chair.

The officer strode forward and holding a revolver to his temple, he fired.

The boy, for he was merely seventeen years old, cried out only once, calling for his mother.

## Blighty Wound

He's got a Blighty One, the lucky sod.

This morning, four fingers of his right hand were blown off, but otherwise, he's fine.

They'll patch him up and send him back to Blighty.

No more fighting for him.

I expect they'll find something for him to do, perhaps they'll give him an office job, but whatever happens, he'll be home with his family, while we take our chances in the trenches.

I want to go home so much I'd shoot my own hand off, but the penalty for self-inflicted wounds is execution by firing squad.

Oh, for a Blighty wound!

## Christmas Truce

We thought it was a trap, but the Germans
walking across No Man's Land with a white flag
were unarmed. We climbed out of our trench
and met them half way. They wished us 'Merry
Christmas', offering us schnapps and sausage.
We shared rum and plum pudding with them
and after talking a while, someone found a ball,
and we piled up grey and khaki coats together to
make goal posts.

Of course, it had to end. The officers
ordered us back to our line.

Tomorrow, our new friends will become
our enemy again and we will shoot to kill.

# My Grandfathers

Morris Jacobs (1899-1956) and Edward Thomas Kentish (1895-1959) were my grandfathers.

During World War One, Morris Jacobs served in the Royal Navy, Service Number SS116575, and Edward Kentish belonged to the Machine Gun Corps, Regimental Number 136693.

Both men survived the war and came home to their families.

Sadly, Edward died when I was about one year old and Morris died three years later, so I don't remember either of them and don't know what they experienced during the war.

I can only imagine their horror when they discovered twenty-one years later that we were at war with Germany again.

# Trench Raid

It takes a certain type of bloke to go on a trench raid.

Our officer knows which of the lads to choose. He knows those of his men who might have used their fists first, and thought later, before they joined up.

To some men, violence is second nature.

Those men blacken their faces at night or put on balaclavas. Then, armed with perhaps a knife, knuckle-dusters, a pistol, or possibly a selection of weapons, they creep across No Man's Land under cover of darkness to the enemy lines to gather intelligence, take prisoners and generally cause havoc.

Like pirates.

## Studio Portraits

I've set up a photographic studio in the town
where the troops who've been fighting on the
Front Line, come for a break.

Mostly, I take portraits of soldiers.

They want pictures of themselves dressed
smartly in uniform, to send to their families.

Once they've chosen a backdrop I
position them either in groups or individually,
as they want.

With shoulders back, chests puffed out
and hands clasped behind them, they pose,
staring steadily into my lens.

I'm doing a roaring trade but I have many
photographs that still need to be collected.

The pile grows larger day by day.

## Carrier Pigeon

He carries the wicker basket carefully so as not to shake the precious cargo.

The homing pigeon grows restless, eager to spread her cramped wings and take to the skies. She has made many trips before, carrying vital messages from the front, to headquarters.

She will travel at impressive speeds, covering large distances and finding her loft, even though it may have been moved to a new location.

He holds the bird between his hands, speaking encouragingly.

The message is attached and secure.

Now he must release her and pray the enemy's bullets do not find their mark.

God speed.

## My Bible

The bible my sister sent me smells like home,
even though it's covered in mud.

I'm up to my knees in muddy water, so,
at first, I didn't want to open my bible, for fear of
making it dirty.

But what's the point of having the Good
Book and not reading it?

You can tell where my favourite passages
are because those pages are covered in muddy
fingerprints.

I read and reread those chapters, trying to
find hope, trying to find answers, trying to find
comfort.

But peace only comes when I close my
eyes, breathe in, and smell home.

## Last Moments

He grips my hand tightly. I can see the anguish in his eyes.

We joined up together.

We have consecutive regimental numbers.

But our time together is nearly over.

My wounds are severe and I know I cannot live much longer.

There's nothing he can do for me except offer words of false encouragement.

We both know there's no hope.

But I'm not dying fast enough.

He won't leave me until I've gone, but he needs to go now or he won't make it.

One of us must survive.

I close my eyes.

Where are you death?

Take me now!

## Censored Letters

…I'm sorry this letter is so brief, dearest, but the truth is, I've been quite busy.

I'd only just started writing to you when the orderly arrived with about a hundred letters for me to censor.

My heart went into my boots!

But, of course, you know, dearest, that I have to read each one in case they're intercepted and give away something vital.

Well, I'm happy to say that I've read and signed each one, after concealing certain sentences in blue pencil.

And they're now on their way to Blighty.

So, dearest, I've returned to my letter to you…

## My Parcels

I don't believe it!

Another parcel has gone missing!

How many times do I have to tell them at home to use the correct address?

There are so many of us on the Front with the same surname, they can't blame the postal service.

Would you believe I've just been handed a letter asking me whether I received a parcel containing supplies?

No, I *didn't*!

And do you know why? Because I can't make them understand they need to address my parcels *correctly*.

I'm half-starved and they send me food that goes to some other fellow with the same name.

# The News

When Ma wrote to me about our army's
'glorious victories', I thought she was simply
looking on the bright side, but this newspaper
clipping she's sent explains why she thinks it's
all going so well here on the Front.

I don't know where the reporter got his
information from, but he hasn't spoken to
anyone who's actually been here.

It's true the enemy has suffered great
losses, but so have we.

And as for glorious victories!

There have been no victories.

And there is nothing glorious about
trench warfare.

But I'll let it be.

It's best Ma believes it's true.

# Hot Food

Each night, I fantasise about sitting down at a table spread with all sorts of wonderful food.

Roast beef and Yorkshire pudding, Mum's shepherd's pie, lamb stew and dumplings.

When I get home, I will only eat food that is hot.

Here in the trenches, we get tinned bully beef and stale bread. And that's better than nothing, but I long for something hot that will fill my belly.

Yesterday, someone from the rest camp brought us hot soup in a special container that he carried on his back.

Oh, how marvellous it was to have something warm to eat!

## Unexpected Gifts

This morning at breakfast time, a delivery of parcels arrived at the Front.

Each lad received a box or packet from home and it wasn't until they had all been handed out that we realised there was still a pile of parcels left.

And then the penny dropped.

They were parcels for the lads who hadn't made it. Their families hadn't received the dreadful news, when the contents of each gift was lovingly wrapped.

We divided into twos and threes and shared them out as evenly as possible, without knowing what they contained.

Anything personal will be sent back home.

## The Souvenir

When this bloody war is over, I never want to
think of it again.

    The other lads collect souvenirs which
they send home in parcels or take with them
when they're on leave.

    They gather up all sorts of things like cap
badges, belt plates, helmets and weapons.

    Somehow it doesn't seem honourable to
scavenge bits and pieces from a battle field
where good men lost their lives.

    But I've bought one of the beautiful post
cards decorated with silk, that the locals make,
and I am going to send it to my sweetheart.

    That will be my only souvenir.

## At Sea

A glorious victory?

Or a dreadful disaster?

Perhaps it was both.

The British Grand Fleet met the German High Seas Fleet at the Battle of Jutland, in the North Sea, close to Denmark.

During the sixteen hours of battle, the British lost more ships and more men than the Germans.

The German newspapers declared it a German victory.

And yet, the Royal Navy's British Grand Fleet remained in command of the seas and the German High Seas Fleet did not put to sea again during the Great War.

Almost nine thousand British and German sailors lost their lives that day.

# The Mine

It is warm and airless in the main tunnel.

Jim and I had just arrived for our shift when there was a terrific explosion and I was blown backwards, dropping my lamp. I think I must have passed out because I don't remember much after that. When I finally came round, I was in total darkness. I know Jim is somewhere nearby because I can hear him whimpering in pain, but I can't see him.

I try to reach out to him but I can't move my arms.

I am pinned down by rocks and earth.
We are buried alive.

## Peril Below

This ship is carrying a precious cargo of food from the USA to our people in Britain.

Supplies are urgently needed and our safe arrival in port will be cause for celebration. Not only because of our goods, but because we evaded the German U-Boats that patrol the seas.

Their attacks have become more daring, and they even torpedoed and sank a civilian liner the other day. Once struck, the *Lusitania* only took eighteen minutes to go down, taking with it over a thousand people; men, women and children.

Sailing the Atlantic or Mediterranean Seas is like swimming with sharks.

## The U-Boat

Our U-Boat is the ultimate weapon.

Difficult to locate or to attack, we terrorise the seas, unseen and unheard until we choose to make our presence felt.

We bide our time until we have an unsuspecting enemy ship in our sights, and then we unleash our torpedoes, destroying everything in their path.

The life expectancy of a sailor on a U-Boat is very short.

If we sink to the bottom, there is no escape.

The hatch will not open and if it does, we are too deep to swim to the surface.

But it's best not to dwell on that.

# Anzac Spirit

We landed on this Ottoman peninsula eight months ago and have hardly advanced one mile.

Our home has been this trench beneath the cliffs where thousands of our men have died, picked off by Ottoman snipers, or blown up by artillery.

In the intense heat, flies swarm over the rapidly decomposing corpses and over the living; driving us insane. Those who survive the guns, succumb to dysentery and other diseases.

This is Gallipoli and a legend is born.

It may have been more of a massacre than a battle but out of the ashes has risen the Spirit of Anzac.

## Many Cultures

Most of the battles in this horrendous war are being waged in Europe, but the soldiers who are fighting have been drawn from all corners of the globe.

As the heads of two colonial empires; Britain and France have called upon their resources and people.

Soldiers fight on the battle fields of northern France and Belgium, having travelled great distances from their homes.

Different uniforms, weapons, customs and languages but they join together to fight the enemy.

'Do not think that this is war. It is not war. It is the ending of the world,' observes one of those men.

# My Brother

It was always obvious I'd never measure up to my brother, Charles.

He is older, taller, cleverer and more handsome than me.

He is the favourite son.

If I sound bitter; I'm not.

He is, indeed, a magnificent man and I admire him greatly.

My parents thrill at the knowledge that he has won awards for bravery on the battle field.

In daring acts, he has rescued fellow soldiers and killed large numbers of the enemy.

I cannot compete with him at home or abroad.

When I join up, I will be compared unfavourably, just as I am at home.

## The Birthday

Today, it's my birthday.

When I woke up in the small hours, I was twenty-one years old for the first time.

Today, thankfully, the lads and I aren't in the trenches. We're resting in a village about a mile from the Front, and when the work's done, we'll celebrate.

We'll eat the birthday cake my Mum sent, drink as much as we can get our hands on, and dance with any mam'selles who care to join us.

Today I will make it my *duty* to enjoy myself.

This may be my last birthday celebration. Who knows if I'll reach twenty-two?

# Great Adventure

Looking back on it, I had it quite good.

But I didn't see it like that at the time.

The future stretched ahead of me, tedious and unfulfilling.

I wanted adventure, I wanted to see the world.

So, I joined up.

I'm in foreign parts now, but the French countryside is very much like our own.

Similar fields, trees and streams.

Except for the shell holes of course.

And as for adventure, I've faced death more times than I care to remember.

Now, what I long for, is to be spared, so I can go home to a quiet life.

## Sacred Way

The Sacred Way is the road leading to the forts at Verdun.

It is barely twenty feet wide, hardly sufficient room for two vans to pass, but without it, thousands of men would perish.

It is the main thoroughfare for vehicles and troops.

Approximately two thirds of the French army will march along this road before the Battle of Verdun is over.

First, Germans will advance, pushing back the French, then fortunes will change and the French will advance, driving back the Germans.

And as the death toll mounts, French soldiers march along the Sacred Way that leads to hell.

## Bled White

One leader announces he will bleed his enemy white.

He plans a bombardment so intense, that it will break the enemy, in body, mind and spirit.

The site chosen is Verdun, a place he believes his enemy will defend to the last man.

The fort at Douaumont is taken and held. Later, the tide turns and the enemy reclaim it. Little is won but so much is lost.

The combined price is over seven hundred thousand men.

Today, the bones of many of those men lie together in an ossuary at Douaumont.

Bodies, and pieces of bodies lie together, forever.

## Shell Shock

Inside my head is a tiny place where I like to hide.

I discovered it when a shell exploded close by and hurling me into the air, it buried me under a pile of earth.

While my mates were digging me out, I found the secret place in my mind and I sheltered in there until they'd dragged me out into the daylight.

There is safety in my special refuge, and escape from the constant noise of bombardment.

I put my hands over my ears, close my eyes and creep into my quiet place.

Let me stay here in peace.

# Lucky Charm

A rabbit's foot has kept me alive.

I have control in a world where death is a random occurrence.

We each have something that we hold, or wear, or do, to keep danger at bay.

Many men have rosaries and crucifixes or other religious symbols which they kiss before battle to let their charm know they need its protection.

Others read the signs in nature; the number of birds, their flight path, cloud formations or the phase of the moon.

I keep my rabbit's foot on a chain round my neck and stroke it regularly to ask for its protection.

# The Poster

It's hard to avoid Lord Kitchener's eyes, they seem to follow wherever you go.

And as for that accusing finger, there's no hiding from its demand.

'Your Country Needs YOU,' it says beneath the uncompromising face.

The word 'YOU', is in capital letters, so there is no doubt at whom it is aimed.

There is no escape from this poster, it appears on many hoardings, windows, omnibuses, trams and commercial vans.

There can't be a man alive in England who hasn't been confronted by that pointing finger.

Some will be driven to enlist, while others will feel guilty and wait.

## My Angel

I've been waiting for so long.

Perhaps no one is coming for me and I will die of thirst, here in a shell hole in No Man's Land.

The sun is sinking fast and soon I will be alone in the darkness, my leg shattered and useless.

I close my eyes so I can't see the light fade, but as the minutes pass, it seems, through closed eyelids, that the brightness is growing.

When I look, there is light all around me, and above me is a figure of purest white.

It opens its wings to protect me.

My Angel.

# Under Age

I gave the recruitment officer a false name and lied about my age.

Now I'm Private Albert Grant, aged nineteen and I'm on my way to Flanders.

I practised in the mirror before I went to the recruitment office, standing tall, pulling back my shoulders and deepening my voice.

I needn't have bothered.

In the end, the officer barely looked at me.

He told me I was just the sort of man the army was looking for.

*He* signed the form and *I* signed the form.

Now I'm a soldier.

There's no going back. I'll be in Flanders, fighting soon.

# Too Large

They were some of the first soldiers to be mobilised at the start of the war as the British Expeditionary Force.

There was no action for some weeks but then, early one morning, the Germans came out of the dense mist.

They successfully fought back, but shortly after, their trench came under attack from behind and they were cut off.

As professional soldiers, they were well trained but the ammunition they'd been given was too large to fit in their rifles.

In the end, not one of the eleven officers survived nor one of the one hundred and eighty men.

## At Rest

Men who are resting away from the trenches often have to take part in hard, physical labour, but it doesn't matter how tired the men are, they will always find the energy to kick a football about, and play a game.

Team sports are encouraged to build a spirit of camaraderie, but some pastimes, such as the gambling game, Crown and Anchor, are officially forbidden.

Although it doesn't stop the Tommies playing it.

Other, more creative men indulge in 'Trench Art', making useful objects out of battlefield debris, such as shell cases, which they fashion into vases and tobacco jars.

## Seven Bakers

One by one, each of my bakers have left and gone to war.

I have a photograph of them standing in the yard, dressed in flat caps and white aprons.

They stare unblinking at the camera, unaware that their days in my bakery are numbered, unaware that a few months later, they will each sign up and leave for France.

I run the bakery with two young lads now.

How long before they join up?

I look at the photograph of the seven bakers in the yard with sadness.

Across each apron is written in red pen, the word "Gone".

## My Vision

We have been at war for so long, and fought so hard, I'm beginning to wonder if I have, in fact, died and gone to Hell.

There is little that makes sense.

Men fight, men die, new men arrive to replace them. They fight, they die...

I have a vision.

So many men will have perished that each side will be reduced to one man.

Those two remaining men climb out of their trenches and approach each other.

They fight with bare hands, with nails, with teeth, until both are mortally wounded.

Then, and only then, will the fighting cease.

## I See

My eyes are heavily bandaged, so I cannot see.

After the explosion, it is doubtful if I shall ever see again.

But I have seen too much.

My mind is imprinted with sights no man should have witnessed.

I see them clearly over and over.

A series of moving images, accompanied by the sound and smells of battle.

I try to think of home, of walks along the beach, of sitting under the giant oak in the garden.

But all I can see are men falling, men dying and explosions everywhere.

The gift of sight is sometimes not a blessing.

## Concert Party

With a skirt, blouse and dainty hat, I look like a lady.

The chaps in the audience whistled and stamped when I came on the makeshift stage and sang my first song.

Nerves almost got the better of me, but once I saw their smiles, I gave it all I had, and you should have heard the applause when I'd finished.

It was worth all the rehearsals to know we were taking the chaps' minds off the war.

For an hour or so, in a barn in France, we sang together and lost ourselves in a world of make believe.

## Safe Below

The end of June 1916 saw intense bombardment of the German trenches near the River Somme.

Surely nothing could possibly have survived such a savage onslaught.

On 01 July 1916, the Allies would simply be able to walk across No Man's Land, take the enemy trenches without resistance, and then advance into German-held territory.

But no one had suspected that the Germans had such strong, nor such deep defences.

As the first wave of British and French troops climbed out of their trenches, they were mown down by machine gun fire.

It was the bloodiest day in British military history.

# Messines Ridge

It was still dark at 3.00am and we couldn't see each others' faces but we could feel the tension.

Those with wrist watches checked them every few seconds until it was time.

At 3.10am, the first mine exploded beneath the enemy lines.

The earth trembled and then huge tongues of flame leapt hundreds of feet in the air, followed by dense columns of smoke.

Sparks shot upwards in an infernal firework display.

This was the signal for the start of the battle.

Eighteen more mines exploded.

And every gun on our front was ready with a shell in the breach.

## A Sunday

Days merge into weeks and weeks merge into months.

For some reason, I have been spared, when so many of the courageous lads I joined up with, are gone.

So many now, that there is no longer time to give each man the burial he deserves.

If indeed, a body can be found.

Many have been torn apart into unrecognisable pieces.

The men I once knew, are replaced by other younger, inexperienced men.

A short while ago, a fellow soldier told me it was Sunday today.

I hadn't realised.

But Sunday is as good a day as any for killing.

# Knitted Comfort

Each sock grows, stitch by stitch and row by row.

We chat while we knit, but our conversation turns repeatedly to our menfolk on the front.

Sometimes there is a lull in the conversation, when sorrow is too great, but the needles never stop.

We can do nothing for our men, except pray and knit.

Pray for their lives and souls, and knit for their comfort.

In each pair of socks that I finish, I tuck a small note to the soldier who will receive them.

It includes a short prayer for his safety, to let him know we care.

## Self-Inflicted Wound

As the enemy soldier thrust at me with his bayonet, I lunged at him with my knife.

My aim was truer.

I stabbed him in the chest, he struck my hand.

A shell, then caught both of us, flinging us into the air.

He was dead, but I crawled back to the trench.

It occurred to me then, that my war was over.

I gave thanks I was alive even if my fingers no longer worked.

At the hospital, the doctor claimed my hand wound was self-inflicted.

Surely my broken nose, cracked ribs and shrapnel wounds should tell him otherwise?

# Red Cross

I awoke from unconsciousness and he was there.

The enemy.

There was no escape, my legs were paralysed and I resigned myself to death, hoping it would be swift.

He held out his water flask and pointed to the red cross on his arm.

I hesitated.

He nodded reassuringly and crouching beside me, he held it to my lips.

'I will get a stretcher,' he said.

I shook my head.

I knew he wouldn't be back.

It was enough that he had given me a drink.

'I *will* be back,' he said pointing to the red cross on his arm.

## The Fallen

How do families find closure when their loved one is killed in battle, in a foreign land?

Soldiers are not repatriated.

They are buried close to where they fall.

At the front, men who once fought bitterly, now lie almost side by side and sometimes together, in mass graves.

And their families cannot gather to mourn or to lay flowers.

They cannot say goodbye or touch the earth under which their loved one lies.

But, it is better to know he has been buried with ceremony and honour on foreign soil, than to know that his body was never found.

## The Armistice

The Great War officially ended with the Armistice of 11 November 1918.

During the final days of the war, the Allied armies pushed the German army back, until it occupied roughly the same position that it had, when it had first engaged in battle with the British forces, in 1914.

Four years of bloodshed and misery.

Four years of death and destruction.

Four years of mothers and fathers losing son after son.

Four years of wives losing husbands, and children their fathers.

Four years of deprivation and hardship on the home front.

Four years when spirits were broken.

For what?

## Forget Never

I stand here now in this field in Picardy, where several years ago, I thought I would die.

Grass now covers the land where once, I lived for days at a time in a waterlogged trench.

Deprived of sleep and deafened by the artillery.

I saw good mates die, blown to unidentifiable pieces, or gunned down in a blaze of bullets.

I overcame fear to climb out of the trench and walk across No Man's Land.

And now, it's as if we had never been.

The trenches and graves have been assimilated into the land.

But I will never forget.

## Postal Service

I've got an important delivery of weapons for the lads at the Front today.

Not rifles, hand grenades or knives.

No, in my cart, I'm carrying something much more powerful than those.

You doubt that these are weapons?

Well, know this! Every word and gift from home raises morale in our troops, bringing them comfort.

Each week, over twelve million letters and one million parcels are delivered to our men.

Average time for a letter to reach the Front?

Two days.

Maintaining channels of communication between fighting men and their families, to keep everyone's spirits up, is our highest priority.

# Best Friend

The Red Cross dog has been trained to ignore dead bodies.

The simple first aid kit and water container he carries in his harness is useless to a corpse.

But a lightly wounded soldier can treat himself with the medical supplies and follow him to safety.

From an unconscious or immobile man, the dog takes a cap or piece of torn clothing and carries it to his handler.

He will then lead stretcher bearers to the wounded soldier, under cover of darkness.

The dog's ability to determine who is alive, despite appearances to the contrary, is better than any man's.

# Looking Back

There were many things I enjoyed about the war.

Not the fighting or killing, of course.

But at other times, it was like being on holiday with the lads.

There was an edge of excitement, as if we were taking part in a boy's adventure.

We laughed, played and protected each others' backs.

Had there been no war, I would have stepped into my father's shoes and lived a life the same as his.

Years of meaningless monotony.

Yes, I miss the war.

Not the fighting and killing of course, but I'd give anything to be back with the lads.

## With Respect

I don't know about other men who served during the Great War, but I don't hate the Hun.

People might find that strange, seeing that I spent four years trying to kill as many as I could.

I'm under no illusions that given the right conditions, one of them would have finished me off too.

But they were just like us.

Men under orders, doing a difficult job.

Not many of us liked it, but that's the way it was.

I saw many acts of barbarism on both sides.

But from time to time, there were glimpses of humanity too.

## Old Soldier

For years, I have not spoken a word about my war.

To have done so, would have brought it back and would have made it real again.

No one can comprehend what life in the trenches was like, unless they experienced it, so what would be the point of trying to describe it?

The sights, the smells, the deafening sound, all defy belief.

And how might my family's opinion of me change if they knew the things I'd done? Or the things I hadn't done?

It's not like my war changed people's opinions.

Else why did World War Two happen?

## Seeking Peace

War can't be converted to peace by simply
signing a treaty.

After four long years of mutilation and
death, I know with all certainty that peace has
been destroyed; it no longer exists.

Before the war, I closed my eyes and saw
velvety blackness. I lay in the cornfield and
listened to the buzz of insects, to birdsong and
the voices of children.

Now, on the inside of my eyelids I see the
faces of men who died.

Heroes, cowards, young men and boys.
War made no distinction.
And my ears are filled with their cries.
Peace? Peace is dead.

# My Plea

Let the words spoken by nations and by individuals be thoughtful and respectful.

Let those words be received generously, without prejudice.

Let the assumption be, that the motive of those words is positive and peaceful, rather than jumping to adverse conclusions.

If there is no doubt the meaning of those words is aggressive, then let us make every possible effort to transform people's hearts to peace.

Let us desire and work towards a world where we value and respect everyone who shares this earth with us.

Let us celebrate the similarities between all members of humankind and ignore any differences.

Printed in Great Britain
by Amazon

44554099R00122